T0322842

RESTAURANT AT THE EDGE OF THE WORLD

THE RESTAURANT AT THE EDGE OF THE WORLD

faber

For Ron, who always wanted to hear more.
– OG

For those learning to find their power.
– KJS

First published in the US in 2024 by Little Bee Books
First published in the UK in 2025 by Faber & Faber Limited
The Bindery, 51 Hatton Garden, London, EC1N 8HN
faber.co.uk

All rights reserved | Printed in Europe
Copyright © Oliver Gerlach and Kelsi Jo Silva, 2024
Text © Oliver Gerlach, 2024 | Illustrations © Kelsi Jo Silva, 2024
Designed by Steph Stilwell | Lettering by Dev Kamath

The right of Oliver Gerlach and Kelsi Jo Silva to be identified as authors of this work has been asserted
in accordance with Section 77 of the Copyright, Designs and Patents Act 1988

This book is sold subject to the condition that it shall not, by way of trade or otherwise, be lent, resold, hired out
or otherwise circulated without the publisher's prior consent in any form of binding or cover other than that in which
it is published and without a similar condition including this condition being imposed on the subsequent purchaser

A CIP record for this book is available from the British Library

ISBN 978-0-571-38160-9

MIX
Paper | Supporting
responsible forestry
FSC® C018236

Printed and bound on FSC® paper in line with our continuing commitment to ethical business practices,
sustainability and the environment. For further information see faber.co.uk/environmental-policy

2 4 6 8 10 9 7 5 3 1

TABLE OF CONTENTS

OH! MORNING, BOSS! DIDN'T SEE YOU THERE.

AH, MY FAVOURITE LITTLE CHEF. CARRY ON.

TRYSIL HELDRITCH.
PROPRIETOR. HEAD CHEF. ICON.

'SCUSE ME, BOSS. GOTTA GET THESE OUT!

NOW, ARE YOU **READY**? THIS IS IT.

6

I COULD LIVE A WILD LIFE OF **ADVENTURE** AND **SWORDPLAY**...

BLRRP?

OH YEAH. THIS IS **SQUILLACE**.

HE'S A DISHWATER ELEMENTAL.

THAT'S WHAT YOU GET WHEN YOU TRY TO CUT A WIZARD OFF AT THE BAR.

YEAH, YOU'RE RIGHT, BUD. I'D MISS THIS PLACE AND MY **FRIENDS** IF I LEFT.

BRBLRMM.

DON'T ASK.

8

I COULD SPEND *HOURS* HERE.

HEY!

SOUP! OVER HERE!

CLARION AND I HAVE BEEN FRIENDS SINCE WE WERE BOTH TINY.

HOW'S IT GOING?

I TRUST THEM WITH MY **LIFE**.

'S ALL GOOD. HERE, I SWIPED SOMETHING FOR YOU.

DON'T TELL ANYONE.

AH, YOU'RE THE **BEST**, PAL!

'NYWAY. 'V' GOT SOMEFFN FOR Y'TOO.

NOW, WHERE DID I PUT IT?

CRASH

CLANK

THERE! I FOUND **THIS** IN THE WOODS.

WHAT...WHAT IS IT?

NO IDEA! BUT I'M SURE IT'LL TASTE GOOD.

ALRIGHT, I'LL SEE WHAT I CAN DO.

OUR TEAMWORK IS...**INFAMOUS.**

CLARION AND I COULD PROBABLY DO ANYTHING IF WE PUT OUR MINDS TO IT.

I'M GOING TO HAVE TO GET BACK FOR THE DINNER SHIFT IN A MINUTE.

BUT THANKS FOR THIS!

YOU ALWAYS HAVE TO GO TO WORK.

CAN'T YOU BLOW IT OFF AND COME AND DO SOMETHING **FUN**?

NOT TODAY. MAYBE SOMETIME LATER, THOUGH?

YEAH, YEAH. EXCUSES!

SAVE ME A PORTION OF WHATEVER YOU MAKE, OKAY?

BYE THEN.

THERE'S ALWAYS SOMETHING ELSE TO DO. SOMEONE ELSE TO TALK TO.

I LOVE IT HERE, BUT MAYBE CLARION'S RIGHT.

WHAT **ELSE** IS OUT THERE?

NOT TODAY, BUD. WE'D BETTER HURRY HOME.

OH **NO.**

14

THAT SMELL. WHAT IS IT? IT'S **AMAZING.**

IT'S A POT, INNIT?

I'LL TAKE ONE, PLEASE. WHAT'S IN IT?

'ERE, MESTON! WHAT'S IN TODAY'S POT?

THAT WIGGLY THING WE FOUND IN THE SWAMP. ER, AND SOME OTHER STUFF TOO.

FENSTON! **CAREFUL!** YOU'RE SPILLING STUFF ON ME!

SORRY, MESTON!

COME ON, MOVE US DOWN THE OTHER END. I NEED TOPPINGS.

THANKS!

THIS IS **INCREDIBLE**!

SPICES AND SUGAR, INNIT? GOOD GOBLIN HOME COOKING.

LOOK, I'VE GOT TO GO. BUT THANKS!

MY PLEASURE!

NO, IT'S MINE!

BONG BO

OH, **SORRY**, BOSS. DIDN'T REALISE YOU WERE THERE.

OH, DON'T WORRY ABOUT IT. YOU KNOW YOU'RE MY FAVOURITE, SOUP.

QUICK HEADS UP, THOUGH. WE'RE GOING TO BE A BIT SHORT-HANDED TONIGHT. CYTHERA AND RADOLF ARE OFF.

YOU'LL BE IN CHARGE.

IT'LL BE **FINE**.

AREN'T **YOU** ON THE WORK SCHEDULE FOR TONIGHT?

YOU'LL BE BRILLIANT, CHEF. I'M SURE OF IT.

I...I SUPPOSE SO?

I **KNEW** I COULD RELY ON YOU, CHEF!

I'LL BE BACK LATER!

YOU'RE MY **FAVOURITE** FOR A REASON, CHEF!

DO ME PROUD!

I'M...IN CHARGE?

AFTERNOON, SOUP. I HEAR **YOU'RE** IN CHARGE TONIGHT?

THAT'S RIGHT, FARLING!

WHERE'S THE BOSS? HE'S BEEN IN LESS AND LESS LATELY.

DUNNO, BUT HE'S NOT HERE.

WHAT ON EARTH IS **THAT**?

NO IDEA!

CLARION FOUND IT IN THE FOREST.

I SHOULD HAVE KNOWN **THEY'D** BE INVOLVED.

22

OH.

OH, THIS MIGHT WORK.

HOW ABOUT THAT?

LET'S GO WITH...
HOT SPICED FOREST SURPRISE, GOBLIN-STYLE.

THAT'LL DO.

COOKING HAS BEEN MY **ENTIRE LIFE** FOR AS LONG AS I CAN REMEMBER.

NOBODY KNOWS **WHERE** I CAME FROM.

I WAS JUST...**THERE** ONE DAY, ABANDONED IN THE BIG SOUP POT.

BLUP?

AND I'VE BEEN HERE EVER SINCE.

I'M NOT SURE **ANYONE** HAS EVER HAD SO MANY PARENTS.

HEY, **ROLKO!** COME AND TASTE THIS!

WHOA! THIS IS **GOOD**. KIND OF...SWEET? WHAT IS IT?

INGREDIENTS FROM CLARION; **IDEAS** FROM SOME OF THE MARKET LADS.

WHAT DO YOU THINK? SHOULD I ADD IT AS A **SPECIAL** FOR TONIGHT?

AND CHANGE THE BOSS'S MENU? ARE YOU **MAD**?

29

COME ON, BACK TO WORK! I DON'T PAY YOU TO STAND AROUND AND DO NOTHING!

WHAT. IN ALL THE HELLS. IS **THAT?**

34

JUST TRY IT, BOSS. PLEASE!

AND WHY SHOULD I DO THAT?

BECAUSE IT'S GOOD! PLEASE, I KNOW—

NO, YOU DON'T. THIS IS A **DISGRACE**.

YOU'RE **NOTHING**.

I TAKE YOU IN, GIVE YOU A **HOME** AND A **LIFE**, AND THIS IS HOW YOU REPAY ME?

YOU'RE ONLY HERE BECAUSE I ALLOW IT. I COULD **END** YOU. ALL OF YOU.

CLEAR?

YES.

GOOD KID. I *LIKE* YOU, YOU KNOW. YOU'RE USUALLY SO RELIABLE.

AH!

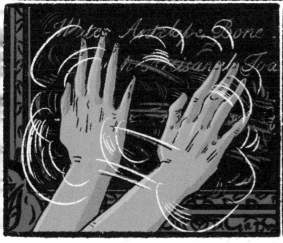

OH.

HE DIDN'T EVEN **TRY** IT.

J.P.

Salad of R

Cheeses an

- Tart of Cly

Wild

- Water Art.

FIRST TIME GETTING CHEWED OUT LIKE THAT? DON'T FEEL TOO BAD ABOUT YOURSELF. HE'S DONE THAT TO MOST OF US.

JUST NOT USUALLY WHEN YOU'RE HERE.

RECENTLY, SOMETIMES, THE BOSS JUST...

...GETS LIKE THAT.

WAIT, HE TREATS THE REST OF YOU THAT WAY?

HE'S NOT GOING TO GET AWAY WITH BEING LIKE THAT FOR LONG.

IT'S BEEN A **LONG WEEK**.

WORKING IN A KITCHEN MEANS THAT **DAYS OFF** ARE RARE.

CHAPTER TWO:
THE STREET

BUT WHEN YOU **FINALLY** GET ONE? IT'S AN OPPORTUNITY LIKE NO OTHER.

COME ON, SQUILLACE. TIME TO GO, BUD.

'HE DID **WHAT**?!'

40

YOU'VE GOT **FRIENDS**. YOU'RE UNBEATABLE.

WE'RE UNBEATABLE.

MAYBE YOU'RE RIGHT.

I **KNOW** I'M RIGHT. I'M **ALWAYS** RIGHT.

HEY, LOOK. D'YOU WANT TO DO **DINNER** TONIGHT?

YOU LOOK LIKE YOU NEED A DISTRACTION, AND I HAVEN'T SEEN YOU **ALL WEEK**.

YEAH. I'LL SEE YOU TONIGHT, THEN?

OF COURSE. YOU KNOW WHAT I LIKE!

YOU JUST LEAVE THAT TO ME!

HELDRITCH GAVE ME A **HOME**. RAISED ME AS PART OF THE **TEAM**. THE **FAMILY**.

I **OWE** HIM FOR THAT...

...DON'T I?

WHERE WOULD I BE WITHOUT HIM?

HEY!

SORRY!

WHAT'S THIS?

I MADE THAT!

HE'S **STOLEN** IT! HE TOOK MY DISH!

'TRYSIL HELDRITCH'S FAMOUS FOREST SURPRISE'?

'YOU ALRIGHT, KID? YOU LOOK DOWN.'

I KNOW THINGS HAVE BEEN *HARD* RECENTLY, BUT—

OH, THIS AIN'T RECENT. MAYBE HE'S *WORSE* NOW, BUT HE'S BEEN A *SLIMEBAG* FOR YEARS.

FIRST TIME GETTING ON HIS BAD SIDE?

ALL 'IS SIDES ARE BAD. HALF THE MARKET'S GOT A STORY ABOUT OL' TRYSIL.

YOU JUST AIN'T SEEN WHAT HE'S *REALLY LIKE* BEFORE.

SORRY YOU HAD TO FIND OUT LIKE THIS, KID.

TAKE THIS. MAYBE IT'LL HELP YOU FEEL BETTER.

ON THE HOUSE.

WE DON'T GOT A HOUSE, FENSTON.

ON THE CART, THEN. SHUT UP, MESTON.

SO, YOU'RE **NOT** ONE OF HIS GOONS?

NO. I GUESS I WORK FOR HIM, BUT . . .

OH, I'M SORRY, LOVE. IS HE TREATING YOU BADLY?

HE'D NEVER LET ME **NEAR** HIS KITCHEN. BUT I'VE *HEARD* THINGS.

YOU'RE NOT ALONE, LOVE. NOT AT ALL.

'NOBODY WANTS FOOD FROM A HOLE,' HE SAID.

'GO BACK UNDERGROUND.' I WON'T FORGET THAT.

BUT I'VE SEEN NOODLES LIKE THIS ON THE MENU—

OH, HE WANTS THE *IDEAS*, JUST NOT THE *PEOPLE*.

HE'D CLAIM TO HAVE INVENTED WALKING IF HE THOUGHT HE COULD MAKE A PROFIT OFF IT.

I HAVE *NO IDEA* WHAT THAT MEANS.

MAYBE HE HAD A SOUL ONCE, BUT THERE'S NONE LEFT NOW.

IT'S A MIRACLE HE HAS ANY STAFF LEFT, CARRYING ON LIKE THAT.

YOU KNOW HE GOT THE TOWN COUNCIL TO SHUT MY BIG SHOP DOWN?

AFRAID OF ANY COMPETITION, HE IS.

BUT THESE LOOK SO GOOD!

OH, THEY ARE. BUT SELLING THEM ON THE *STREET* WHILE HE LORDS IT OVER US? IT'S NOT WHAT THEY DESERVE.

YOU'RE *FINE*, UP THERE IN *HIS* RESTAURANT, DOING YOUR THING IN FRONT OF EVERYONE.

MAYBE **ALL OF US** DESERVE BETTER. WE CAN DO SO MUCH MORE. TOGETHER.

LOOKS LIKE EVERYONE ELSE IS ON BREAK.

THAT'S GOOD. MEANS I CAN USE THE **GOOD** KITCHEN WITHOUT GETTING IN THE WAY.

I NEED TO COOL OFF BEFORE DINNER.

HOW COULD I NOT *SEE*?

I'M SUCH AN **IDIOT**.

THERE WE GO. I HOPE CLARION'S READY FOR A **TREAT**!

OH, DON'T WORRY ABOUT *THAT*. MONEY WON'T BE A PROBLEM AFTER *THE STREET*.

THAT'S THE STREET BY *HELDRITCH* TO YOU.

ONCE THE MARKET'S FLATTENED AND WE'VE GOTTEN RID OF THOSE **PESTS**, YOU'LL BE FINE.

NO... THEY'RE GOING TO DESTROY THE MARKET?

I'VE GOT TO GET OUT OF HERE **NOW**.

THESE GUYS MAKE MY SKIN CRAWL.

HEY! WHO'S THAT SPYING ON US?

EH? OH, THAT'S JUST SOUP.

COME AND JOIN US FOR A LITTLE DRINK, CHEF!

GOTTA RUN, BOSS! SORRY!

YOU'RE NO FUN. YOUR LOSS, KID!

THAT WAS CLOSE.

I'M GOING TO HAVE **SO MANY** GREAT TEXTILES ON SALE NEXT WEEK. YOU'D BETTER COME AND CHECK THEM OUT!

I'M SO READY TO—

CLARION.

CLARION.

OH! FOOD!

DINNER'S READY, **KNUCKLEHEAD**.

LOOK DOWN THERE. DON'T YOU GET *JEALOUS* OF THOSE GUYS? SPENDING *WEEKS* OUT THERE ON ADVENTURES?

I WANT TO SEE THE *WORLD*, SOUP. ALL OF IT. DON'T YOU EVER FEEL *TRAPPED* IN YOUR LITTLE KITCHEN?

I...

I...STILL DON'T KNOW.

COME ON. WE COULD **RUN AWAY** TOGETHER. GET OUT OF HERE, AWAY FROM IT ALL.

I CAN'T.

LOOK, YOU SAID THIS MORNING, ALL IS **NOT** WELL IN SOUP-LAND.

SCREW TRYSIL HELDRITCH. YOU DON'T NEED HIM OR HIS RESTAURANT. LET'S HAVE AN ADVENTURE!

I CAN'T JUST CUT AND RUN WHEN THINGS GET HARD. THAT'S NOT HOW **KITCHENS** WORK.

BUT YOU'RE **MISERABLE!**

I KNOW! I **KNOW** I'M MISERABLE! BUT IF I QUIT, THEN I'M JUST LEAVING MY *FAMILY* AND MY *HOME* BEHIND AND MAKING **EVERYTHING** SOMEONE ELSE'S PROBLEM!

OKAY, OKAY. SORRY, PAL. I SHOULDN'T HAVE PUSHED.

SORRY.

IT DOESN'T MATTER HOW BADLY ANYONE SCREWS UP, WE GET BACK UP, TIDY THE MESS, AND WE'RE READY THE NEXT MORNING.

THE RESTAURANT STILL HAS TO BE ABLE TO OPEN. EVERY DAY.

SO I'M NOT GOING **ANYWHERE**.

I DON'T **WANT** TO LEAVE.

I COULD CHANGE FOOD IN THIS CITY. I COULD MAKE SOMETHING **SPECIAL**.

SO MANY OF US COULD, IF HE'D JUST LET US **SHOW PEOPLE**!

I WANT TO MAKE THINGS BETTER FOR **EVERYONE**, NOT JUST FOR ME.

WOW. WHERE DID **THAT** COME FROM?

SORRY. LET'S JUST EAT.

WELL, I WON'T OBJECT TO THAT.

BUT COME ON. WHAT'S **WRONG**, PAL?

DID SOMETHING ELSE HAPPEN TODAY?

HOW DO I PUT THIS INTO WORDS?

YOU KNOW WHAT I WAS SAYING ABOUT THE **BOSS** THIS MORNING?

IT'S SO MUCH **WORSE** THAN THAT.

HE'S JUST TAKING *ADVANTAGE* OF YOU!

TELLING YOU HOW MUCH YOU *OWE* HIM WHILE HE *STEALS* FROM YOU?

PROFITING OFF YOUR WORK LIKE THAT?

THAT'S *ABUSIVE*.

I'M GOING TO GO AND GIVE THAT *SLIMEBALL* A PIECE OF MY MIND! MAYBE I'LL FEED HIM HIS OWN *APRON!*

YOU CAN'T! HE'LL RUIN US BOTH!

HE'S *RICH* AND *FAMOUS* AND *EVERYONE* LOVES HIM.

WELL, ALMOST EVERYONE.

AND WE'RE JUST *TWO WEIRD KIDS* WITHOUT A PLAN.

NOBODY CAN BE THAT *ARROGANT* WITHOUT EVER MAKING A MISTAKE.

HE'LL SLIP UP, AND PEOPLE WILL SEE WHO HE *TRULY* IS.

I DON'T THINK WE'VE GOT TIME TO WAIT FOR A MISTAKE.

THEN WE NEED TO DO SOMETHING *NOW*. WE NEED TO SHOW EVERYONE HE'S *NOT* ALL THAT.

BUT HOW?

WE'LL FIGURE SOMETHING OUT.

WE ALWAYS DO.

CHAPTER THREE:
RECIPE FOR DISASTER

I CAN'T ALLOW MY BOSS TO **DESTROY** THE MARKETPLACE.

I'M GOING TO WATCH HIM LIKE A HAWK.

EVEN **HELDRITCH** HAS TO HAVE A WEAKNESS.

AND WE'RE GOING TO USE THAT TO **SAVE** THE MARKET FROM HIM.

NEARLY READY OVER HERE! HOW'S THE SAUCE?

EVENING, GANG! IT'S BUSY OUT THERE!

THIS IS IT.

ORDER UP FOR TABLE TWO!

WHERE ARE THE SERVERS?

NONONONONO!

THERE'S A **SAYING** WE HAVE IN THE KITCHEN.

NOBODY WANTS TO BE IN THE WEEDS.

BUT SOMETIMES, IT JUST HAPPENS.

AND OTHER TIMES **SOMEONE ELSE** PUSHES YOU INTO THE WEEDS.

LOOKS LIKE YOU'VE GOT THIS COVERED!

I'LL BE IN THE TAVERN IF ANYONE NEEDS ME.

AND **THAT** IS THE SIGNAL FOR DINNERTIME. REGULAR AS CLOCKWORK.

HE'S THE BOSS. WHAT CAN WE DO?

TAP TAP

THANKS! 'S **COLD** OUT THERE!

HEYA, SOUP! AND THE WHOLE GANG!

HOP!

KEEP IT DOWN! YOU KNOW YOU'RE NOT SUPPOSED TO BE HERE AFTER HOURS.

OH RIGHT, YEAH, SORRY.

ANY DINNER LEFT? I'M **STARVING.**

74

IT'S NOT JUST US, AND I'VE HAD **ENOUGH**.

WE CAN'T MAKE NAMES FOR OURSELVES WITH HIM TAKING THE CREDIT...

...AND WE CAN'T GO ANYWHERE ELSE, BECAUSE EVERYONE KNOWS HIM. EVERYONE *LOVES* GOOD OLD CELEBRITY CHEF **TRYSIL HELDRITCH**.

I USED TO LOOK *UP* TO HIM. I THOUGHT HE CARED ABOUT THE FOOD HE MADE AND ABOUT US.

BUT HE *NEVER* COOKS ANYTHING HIMSELF. HE'S A FRAUD. A CHEAT. A **LIAR**. AND I THINK WE'D ALL BE BETTER OFF WITHOUT HIM.

YOU MEAN...YOU WANT TO GET RID OF THE BOSS?

I'M NOT... I DON'T...

HE'S TAKING ADVANTAGE OF **ALMOST EVERYONE** IN THE CITY **AND** BEYOND ITS WALLS!

SOMEONE'S GOT TO DO SOMETHING ABOUT IT. WHY NOT US?

SLAM!

WHAT DO YOU ALL THINK YOU'RE DOING? I DON'T PAY YOU TO SIT AROUND AND DO NOTHING!

EATING? YOU'RE **STEALING** FROM ME? THIS IS MINE.

YOU THINK YOU CAN JUST *TAKE MY FOOD?* THAT I PAID FOR?

GET OUT. YOU'RE **DONE** HERE.

BUT—

DON'T TALK BACK. GET **OUT** OF MY RESTAURANT BEFORE I MAKE YOU.

HEY!

WHAT? DO **YOU** WANT TO LOSE YOUR JOB TOO?

WHY ARE YOU DOING THIS? DOES TREATING YOUR STAFF LIKE THIS MAKE YOU FEEL BIG?

CARE TO REPEAT THAT, **KID**?

YOU'RE TREATING **US** LIKE DIRT SO **YOU** CAN FEEL BIG AND IMPORTANT.

BUT WE'RE NOT DIRT. WE'RE **PEOPLE**. ALL OF US. AND WE'RE NOT STANDING FOR THIS ANYMORE.

OH, YOU'RE **NOT**, ARE YOU? WELL, WHAT ARE YOU GOING TO DO ABOUT IT?

THIS IS MY KITCHEN. MY RESTAURANT. MY CITY. MY **WORLD**.

IF I WILLED IT, YOU'D NEVER WORK AGAIN. ANYWHERE. THIS WHOLE TOWN IS UNDER MY THUMB, AND YOU'RE **NOTHING**. ALL OF YOU.

SO GO ON THEN, SOUP. WHAT DID YOU WANT TO SAY?

MAYBE THAT'S TRUE. BUT, YOU KNOW, *CHEF*, NONE OF US HAVE SEEN YOU COOK ANYTHING **NEW** IN A LONG TIME.

YOU'RE REALLY THAT BIG A DEAL?

SHOW US YOU'RE NOT OUT OF IDEAS. SHOW EVERYONE WHAT YOU'RE *REALLY* MADE OF. ALL WE'VE HEARD ARE THREATS.

PROVE IT.

LET'S MAKE A SHOW OF IT. **COOKING CONTEST**. ME AND YOU.

WE PLAY FOR **EVERYTHING**.

OR ARE YOU AFRAID YOU CAN'T BEAT A **KID** LIKE ME? A NOTHING?

SCARED?

OF COURSE NOT. BUT WHY WOULD I LOWER MYSELF TO THAT?

YOU ALL KNOW WHAT I'VE DONE FOR THIS TOWN. GUIDING IT, SUPPORTING IT, FOR **CENTURIES**.

NOD

LOOKS TO ME LIKE YOU'RE **SCARED**, PAL.

FINE. IT CAN BE **PUBLICITY** FOR MY **NEW PLACE**. THE JUDGES WILL BE THE **TOWN COUNCIL**. MY TOWN COUNCIL.

AND WHEN I WIN, YOU'RE **OUT**. GO FIND ANOTHER CITY AND SEE IF ANYONE TAKES YOU IN LIKE I DID.

LIKE WE DID—

SHUT UP.

YOU'VE GOT THREE WEEKS, SOUP, AND THEN YOU'RE **FINISHED**. A SHAME, REALLY. YOU USED TO BE MY **FAVOURITE**.

AND IF I WIN, YOU'LL **STEP DOWN**. NO MORE 'THE STREET: BY HELDRITCH,' NO MORE EMPIRE BUILDING.

YOU LET THE REST OF US HAVE THE SPOTLIGHT.

IF YOU WIN? DON'T MAKE ME LAUGH.

WE'LL SEE ABOUT THAT.

DO WE HAVE A DEAL?

YOU'VE MADE A **HUGE** MISTAKE, KID.

WAIT. WHAT'S STOPPING YOU FROM *IGNORING* THE TERMS? HOW DO I **KNOW** YOU'LL STICK TO THE AGREEMENT?

GUYS? I THINK I MIGHT HAVE GONE A BIT TOO FAR.

HEY, NO—

HOW CAN I *POSSIBLY* BEAT HIM?

MAYBE HE'S RIGHT. I **AM** NOTHING.

AND ONCE I'M **GONE**, HE'LL TAKE IT OUT ON ALL OF YOU.

HEY, NOW. MAYBE YOU WERE A *BIT* IMPETUOUS, BUT THAT **NEEDED** TO BE DONE.

WE'VE ALL SEEN HE'S GETTING HARDER AND HARDER TO BEAR. THANKS FOR **STANDING UP** TO HIM.

MAYBE HE CAN BEAT *YOU*, BUT HE CAN'T BEAT ALL OF US IF WE WORK TOGETHER.

WE'RE WITH YOU.

ENOUGH IS ENOUGH.

IF ALL I THINK ABOUT IS MY *OWN* FOOD, I CAN'T DEVELOP BEYOND MY CURRENT LIMITS.

WE'RE GOING TO NEED TO PUT TOGETHER A **TEAM**.

THIS IS BIGGER THAN ME. IT'S BIGGER THAN THIS ENTIRE **KITCHEN**.

YOU'RE NOT GOING TO FIND A BETTER RANGE OF PERSPECTIVES ANYWHERE ELSE.

YOU WANT TO *TRAIN*? GET THE *MARKET* ON YOUR SIDE.

I DON'T THINK IT'S GOING TO BE THAT SIMPLE.

WHY SHOULD I BELIEVE YOU? **KNOCKING DOWN** THE MARKET? I'VE NEVER HEARD ANYTHING MORE ABSURD.

BUT—

SOUNDS LIKE A **KITCHEN** PROBLEM TO ME.

TEACH **YOU** TO COOK? THIS SOUNDS LIKE A TRICK.

NO, I'M NOT GOING TO JOIN YOUR **TEAM**. SHOVE OFF.

THIS ISN'T GOING TO WORK.

WAIT, I'VE GOT AN *IDEA*. DON'T GO ANYWHERE.

HEY! I BROUGHT **MUM** AND **DAD** TO HELP OUT.

ALWAYS HAPPY TO LEND A HAND FOR WEE CLARION'S PALS!

ALRIGHT, **DAD**, THAT'S ENOUGH 'WEE CLARION', THANKS.

CLARION SAYS YOU'RE PUTTING TOGETHER A CRACK TEAM OF COOKS?

COME ON, LET'S GO AND MAKE EVERYONE SEE SENSE!

I **LOVE** CLARION'S PARENTS. THEY'VE ALWAYS ACCEPTED EVEN THE MOST **ABSURD** OF OUR ADVENTURES.

LIKE THAT ONE TIME WITH THE **FLOCK OF BIRDS** AND THE **CURED HAM** . . .

BUT YOU **DON'T** NEED TO HEAR ABOUT **THAT**.

...SO, YOU KNOW HOW I'VE BEEN WORKING THIS MARKET SINCE FOREVER, RIGHT?

OF COURSE. WHAT CAN I DO FOR YOU?

BAD NEWS, I'M AFRAID.

MARKET'S IN TROUBLE.

IN TROUBLE? WHAT IS IT **THIS** TIME?

YEAH. THE **MANTICORE'S** AT IT AGAIN. CAN WE COUNT ON YOU TO HELP OUT?

ANYTHING FOR YOU TWO!

THERE. WE'LL GET THEM ALL ON YOUR SIDE. DON'T YOU WORRY.

THANKS!

THERE'S **NOBODY** I'D RATHER HAVE IN MY CORNER.

AND A LOT OF **THEM** DON'T LIKE **YOU**, FOR GOOD REASON. THE MANTICORE HAS DONE A LOT OF HARM ROUND HERE.

YOU DON'T HAVE TO LIKE EACH OTHER; YOU JUST HAVE TO GET ALONG WELL ENOUGH TO DO THE JOB.

DON'T PATRONISE ME.

THIS IS GOING TO BE A **LONG** FEW WEEKS.

ALL OF YOU! **STOP IT!**

HALF THE MARKET THINKS THE **COOKS** ARE SPIES FOR HELDRITCH.

HALF THE COOKS THINK THE **MARKET** IS BENEATH THEM.

WE'RE **NEVER** GOING TO BEAT HELDRITCH FIGHTING LIKE THIS.

OH NO. WHAT DO I DO **NOW**?

CAN YOU JUST STOP FIGHTING? *PLEASE?*

I *REALLY* NEED YOUR HELP.

WE'VE GOT A CHANCE TO MAKE A **DIFFERENCE**. TO SHAKE OFF HELDRITCH'S GRIP OVER OUR LIVES.

I JUST NEED TO *OUTDO* HIM IN A COOKING CONTEST.

I'M GOING TO NEED YOUR **HELP** TO DO THAT.

YOU ALL HAVE **DIFFERENT** OUTLOOKS ON FOOD, AND WE CAN ALL **LEARN** FROM EACH OTHER.

YOU CALL THAT A JULIENNE? THROW THAT OUT AND DO IT AGAIN.

IT'S ONLY BEEN **TWO DAYS** SINCE I CHALLENGED HIM TO THE **COOK-OFF**, AND HE'S ALREADY UNBEARABLE.

I'M GOING TO THE TAVERN. DON'T BOTHER ME.

BUT IT'S ALMOST LUNCH SERVICE!

CHAPTER FOUR: IN THE WEEDS

SOUP CAN TAKE CARE OF IT.

HE'S TAKING HIS TEMPER OUT ON **ALL** OF US.

BUT **MOSTLY** HE'S TAKING IT OUT ON **ME**.

WE'LL HAVE TO GET THROUGH THIS TO SAVE THE MARKET. BUT EVEN WITH MY FRIENDS HELPING, I'M SO **TIRED**.

FLOP

YEAH, BUDDY. I'LL TAKE A SHOWER IN A MINUTE. JUST LET ME REST A BIT.

'YOU LOOK **AWFUL**.'

LIKE, PROPERLY AWFUL.

THANKS, REALLY APPRECIATED.

NO SIGN OF THE BOSS OR CYTHERA. LOOKS LIKE IT'S GOING TO BE A ROUGH DAY.

HE'S DOING THIS ON PURPOSE.

EVEN IF IT KILLS ME.

BUT I **WON'T** LET HIM WEAR ME DOWN.

CAN'T I JUST TAKE A BREAK FOR A BIT?

NO TIME FOR THAT! I'VE GOT *SOMETHING* THAT'LL CHEER YOU UP, THOUGH.

FOLLOW ME!

ARE YOU READY?

THIS IS THE MOST **BEAUTIFUL** THING I'VE EVER SEEN IN MY LIFE.

SO WHAT DO YOU **THINK**? DAD AND I HAVE BEEN **WORKING** ON THIS NONSTOP. IT'S FOR **YOU**! DO YOU LIKE IT?

YOU DID ALL OF THIS FOR ME?

YEP! CAN'T DEVELOP THE **BEST** DISH IN THE CITY'S HISTORY WITHOUT A **TEST KITCHEN**, CAN YOU?

GET IN THERE! THE **OTHERS** WILL BE HERE **SOON**.

UM, THANKS FOR COMING, EVERYONE.

WHAT WE NEED IS SOMETHING THAT SHOWS THE JUDGES WHO WE ARE AND WHAT WE CARE ABOUT.

BUT ALSO, I WANT TO MAKE SOMETHING *FUN* AND *SURPRISING*.

COOKING SHOULD BE **FUN**.

CLARI! WHAT'S REALLY FRESH AT THE MOMENT, OUT IN THE WOODS?

FISH! *SO MANY* FISH. THEY'RE PRACTICALLY **HOPPING** OUT OF THE RIVER.

RIGHT. LET'S SEE WHAT WE CAN DO WITH *FISH*, THEN.

ON NO! I'VE GOT TO GO, I'M ON SHIFT TONIGHT AGAIN.

ENJOY THE REST OF THE FISH, GUYS!

SORRY! SORRY!

I HOPE YOU'RE NOT **FLAKING OUT** ON US, SOUP!

BOSS SAYS YOU'RE ON SAUTÉ TONIGHT, AND WE'VE GOT SOME *BIG* BOOKINGS. GOOD LUCK?

I'VE BEEN WORKING **SPLIT SHIFTS** ALL WEEK.

I JUST WANT TO **SLEEP**.

WHAT ARE WE TRYING TODAY?

I THOUGHT IT MIGHT BE INTERESTING TO COOK THE FISH IN A CRUST!

WHAT'S THE PASTRY? IT LOOKS GOOD.

JUST A BASIC FLAKY CRUST, BUT THERE ARE SOME *SPICES* IN THERE FOR COLOUR TOO.

YELLOW PEPPER, SOME MILD CHILLIS.

GIVE THAT ABOUT FORTY-FIVE MINUTES. . .

FARLING'S SO GOOD WITH PASTRY.

THIS IS EXCELLENT.

IS THERE ANY MORE?

I'VE GOT A *THOUGHT*. MAY I TRY SOMETHING?

OF COURSE! THAT'S WHAT WE'RE HERE TO DO!

WHAT ARE YOU DOING TO MY **DISH**?

HERE, TRY *THIS*. THE **SALT-CURED SHOREBERRIES** SHOULD GIVE A BIT OF CONTRAST.

YOU NEED SOMETHING *BITTER* TO CUT THE RICHNESS OF A FISH LIKE THAT.

IT'S **TART** AND **SALTY**, BUT THE FISH IS STILL **DISTINCT**.

I LOVE IT.

IT'S THREE IN THE MORNING.

WE WERE COOKING TILL **THREE IN THE MORNING**!

THAT WAS SO MUCH **FUN**.

I'M SO GLAD I DON'T HAVE THE MORNING SHIFT.

WHAM

WHAM

WH

HEY, SOUP! WE NEED YOU IN THE KITCHEN, STAT!

BOSS CHANGED THE SCHEDULE AGAIN! YOU'RE UP!

HE'S TRYING TO **BREAK** ME.

IF WE CAN ADD ENOUGH GELATINE, WE *MIGHT* JUST BE ABLE TO PUT SAUCE INSIDE A PANCAKE.

NOW WE JUST **WAIT** FOR THAT TO GEL.

I'VE NEVER THOUGHT OF THIS BEFORE.

THERE WE GO! SOLID ENOUGH TO WRAP, THEN WHEN WE COOK IT...

ALL THESE PEOPLE ARE SO **CLEVER**. I'VE STILL GOT SO MUCH TO LEARN.

THIS...DOESN'T HAVE ANYTHING TO DO WITH **FISH** THOUGH.

THIS IS **FUN**. DO YOU THINK YOU'VE GOT A CHANCE?

I DUNNO. I'VE LEARNED *SO MUCH* ALREADY THIS WEEK.

BUT EVERYTHING WE'VE MADE HAS ALL BEEN **SEPARATE** IDEAS. WE HAVEN'T EVEN GOT A VAGUE DISH TOGETHER YET.

HEY! BACK AWAY FROM MY STALL!

I'M NOT *TOUCHING* YOUR STALL!

ALL YOU KITCHEN THUGS ARE THE SAME! LIES ALL THE TIME!

WOW, OKAY THEN—

I DON'T WANT TO SEE ANY OF YOU AROUND HERE ANYMORE.

Home Cuisine

YOU'LL DESERVE *EVERYTHING YOU GET* WHEN THIS PLACE GETS **REPLACED**!

THAT'S NOT GOOD.

CAN'T EVERYONE JUST TRY TO GET ALONG?

AREN'T WE ALL ON THE *SAME* SIDE?

LOT OF FOLKS DON'T SEE IT THAT WAY. AND CAN YOU BLAME THEM? THEY'VE GOT *GOOD* REASON FOR A GRUDGE.

A FEW OF THE COOKS AREN'T HELPING MATTERS.

THERE ARE BOOTLICKERS IN *EVERY* KITCHEN, CONVINCED THEY'LL BE *REWARDED* FOR SUCKING UP TO THE BOSS.

SOME PEOPLE LIKE TO FOLLOW THE POWERFUL. WE CAN'T DO MUCH ABOUT THAT.

THERE'S STILL MORE OF *US* THAN THERE ARE OF *THEM*.

I THINK.

HANG ON, WHERE'S ROLKO?

MAYBE HE'S STILL IN BED.

I HOPE HE TURNS UP *SOON*. HE WAS *REALLY* ONTO SOMETHING WITH THAT SAUCE.

DON'T WORRY ABOUT THAT JUST NOW, LOVE. I'VE BROUGHT SOME FRESH BITS FOR US TO TRY.

THESE ARE GOOD, BUT I'VE BEEN *THINKING*.

WE'VE GOT FISH, RICE, PASTRY, SAUCES, FRUIT, PANCAKES... WE HAVE LOTS OF GOOD ELEMENTS BUT WE HAVEN'T GOT A DISH.

WE'RE RUNNING OUT OF TIME. I'VE SEEN TRYSIL COOK FOR YEARS, AND IF WE CAN'T PULL THIS TOGETHER, IT'S ALL OVER FOR SOUP.

SHE'S RIGHT. WE'VE HAD PLENTY OF **IDEAS**, BUT NONE OF THEM GO TOGETHER.

WE CAN'T **AGREE** ON ANYTHING. NONE OF IT WORKS **TOGETHER**.

HEY! ROLKO!

NO! YOU'VE GOT THE WRONG MAN!

GOT YOU! **WHAT** ARE YOU UP TO? **WHY** DIDN'T YOU TURN UP THIS MORNING?

OOF.

I CAN'T *HELP* YOU GUYS ANYMORE. SORRY, SOUP. I REALLY AM.

BUT WHY?

BOSS OFFERED ME A **PAY RISE**. I COULDN'T SAY NO.

I'VE GOT A *FAMILY* TO FEED. I HARDLY SEE THEM ANYWAY, WORKING *KITCHEN HOURS*. I HAD TO TAKE IT.

IS THE WHOLE TOWN FALLING APART BECAUSE OF **ME**?

MAYBE CLARION WAS **RIGHT**. MAYBE I **SHOULD** HAVE JUST CALLED IT QUITS.

I **HATE** THIS.

...I WANT A SNACK.

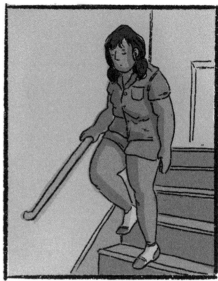

115

117

I'VE *TRIED* TO PLAY NICE. BUT YOU HAVE TO UNDERSTAND THE **POSITION** WE'RE *BOTH* IN.

WE'VE RUN INTO A LITTLE *PROBLEM*.

JUST A *LITTLE* ONE. JUST A *KID*.

'JUST A KID,' AM I? HE'S NOT EVEN TAKING ME SERIOUSLY.

I JUST, UH, NEED A HAND TO REALLY *HUMILIATE* HER.

SCUMBAG.

SO HOW ABOUT IT? JUST *ONE* MORE HIT. THEN I WON'T NEED ANOTHER . . .

NO. WE WILL NOT CONTINUE TO **FEED** YOU LIKE THIS.

COME ON. JUST ONE MORE—

NO. YOU HAVE TAKEN **SO MUCH** FROM US.

AND I'VE GIVEN YOU SO MUCH IN RETURN. WHO IS IT THAT KEEPS YOU **SAFE** OUT THERE?

WITHOUT ME KEEPING THEM BACK, THE TOWNSFOLK WOULD HAVE RAZED YOUR LITTLE **COURTS** YEARS AGO.

REMIND ME WHICH COURT YOU'RE FROM?

OH, RIGHT. I DON'T CARE.

ENOUGH.

I CAN SMELL SO MUCH MORE NOW. I CAN SEE THE FLAVOURS.

THAT KID WON'T KNOW WHAT HIT HER.

YES, THAT'LL DO FOR NOW. YOU MAY GO.

BE OFF WITH YOU. BACK TO YOUR **FOREST**.

KRK

HEH. FOOLS.

WHAT WAS **THAT**?

I HAVE TO GET AWAY BEFORE HE FINDS ME.

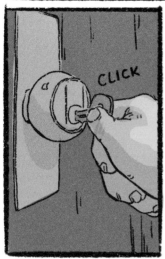

CLICK

WHAT DO YOU THINK? SHOULD I BRING ALL THE PANS?

THIS IS IT.

**CHAPTER FIVE:
OUTSIDE THE BOX**

TAP
TAP
TAP

WURGH?

SOUP?

HEY. SORRY ABOUT
WAKING YOU UP.

BUT YOU
WERE RIGHT.

I *ALWAYS* AM.
BUT WHAT ARE YOU
TALKING ABOUT?

IT'S TIME TO GET
OUT OF TOWN.

COULDN'T THIS WAIT TILL **MORNING?**

I THINK WE SHOULD GO NOW.

WHY WON'T THEY **LISTEN** TO ME?

LOOK, I KNOW I'VE ALWAYS SAID I *DON'T* WANT TO GO ANYWHERE, BUT...

BUT.

CLARION I'VE MADE A *HUGE* MISTAKE, AND I *CAN'T* BEAT HELDRITCH, AND HE'S JUST GOING TO *HURT* EVERYONE I CARE ABOUT AND I *CAN'T* DO THIS ANYMORE!

SOUP. PAL. THAT WAS A *LOT.* SLOW DOWN.

WE CAN GET THROUGH THIS *TOGETHER,* THOUGH. RIGHT?

I THINK I DON'T HAVE A *CHANCE* OF WINNING. I *HAVE* TO GET OUT OF HERE.

AREN'T YOU ALWAYS SAYING WE SHOULD GO ON AN ADVENTURE? COME ON! LET'S GO!

I CAN'T BELIEVE I'M ABOUT TO SAY THIS, BUT...

YOU *CAN'T* RUN AWAY ON AN ADVENTURE. NOT *NOW*. NOT AFTER ALL THIS.

BUT...HE'S GOING TO *RUIN* ME.

NOT IF WE *STOP* HIM.

I'D *LOVE* TO TAKE YOU ON AN ADVENTURE. I REALLY, REALLY WOULD.

BUT RIGHT NOW, WE'VE GOT MORE *IMPORTANT* THINGS TO DO.

I COULDN'T LIVE WITH MYSELF IF I HELPED YOU *DITCH* EVERYONE AND RUN AWAY.

IT WOULDN'T BE *RIGHT*. NOT *NOW*.

BUT I DON'T HAVE A FUTURE IF I STAY. I DON'T.

LOOK, PAL. YOU *KNOW* HOW MUCH I LOVE YOU. PLEASE, JUST *LISTEN* TO ME.

YOU SAID IT YOURSELF. IN THE KITCHEN, YOU *DON'T* JUST DROP EVERYTHING. PEOPLE ARE COUNTING ON YOU.

I'M NOT GONNA LET YOU LET THEM DOWN.

YOU REALLY MEAN THAT?

YEAH. I LOVE GOING OUT THERE AND HAVING FUN, BUT I LOVE **YOU** MORE. AND I KNOW HOW MUCH THAT **KITCHEN** MEANS TO YOU.

THANKS. I KNOW HOW **HARD** IT WAS FOR YOU TO SAY NO TO AN ADVENTURE.

MAYBE YOU'RE **RIGHT**. BUT HOW ARE WE GOING TO FIX THIS?

YOU RECKON HELDRITCH IS GOING TO PLAY **DIRTY**?

THEN MAYBE IT'S TIME FOR **US** TO PLAY DIRTY. HE CAN'T **STOP** US.

...SO, YEAH, IT SOUNDED LIKE HE WAS *BLACKMAILING* SOMEONE.

MAYBE THIS WON'T BE SO BAD AFTER ALL.

IF HE'S BLACKMAILING *ONE* PERSON, WHAT ARE THE CHANCES HE'S DOING IT TO *EVERYONE*?

AND WHAT IF WE COULD *EXPOSE* THAT?

BUT WE DON'T HAVE ANY *PROOF*. NOBODY WOULD BELIEVE ME.

WELL, THEN WE'LL JUST HAVE TO *GET* SOME.

I THINK THIS MIGHT ACTUALLY BE *FUN*.

I KNOW WHAT THAT EXPRESSION MEANS...

I FEEL LIKE A SPY, INFILTRATING ENEMY TERRITORY.

YOU KNOW, I KIND OF THOUGHT HE'D HAVE COME OUT BY NOW.

YEAH...MAYBE WE MISSED HIM?

AND DON'T YOU DARE ASK ME FOR HELP AGAIN!

GO GO GO! DON'T LET HIM GET OUT OF SIGHT!

KEEP IT DOWN! HE'LL HEAR!

NOW, I KNOW YOU HAVE A FEW...*ISSUES* WITH THE PLANS TO REPLACE THE MARKET WITH A NEW RESTAURANT.

BUT WHAT IF THOSE ISSUES... *WENT AWAY?*

AH. WELL, I THINK YOU KNOW YOUR PLANS HAVE *ALWAYS* HAD MY SUPPORT, MR HELDRITCH.

BRIBERY? NO SURPRISES THERE.

I *KNEW* HE WAS A REAL PIECE OF WORK.

BLACKMAIL, BRIBERY, EXTORTION. IT'S BEEN A BUSY DAY FOR THE BOSS!

SO, NOW *WE* KNOW HE'S PULLING ALL SORTS OF NONSENSE, BUT HOW DO WE TELL *OTHERS*?

I MEAN, EVEN IF HE'S PULLING THE BIG STRINGS, HE CAN'T STAND AGAINST THE *WHOLE* TOWN TOGETHER.

WE NEED *EVIDENCE.* AND I STILL WANT TO KNOW WHO IT WAS THAT GAVE HIM *MAGIC.*

ARE *YOU* THINKING WHAT *I'M* THINKING, PAL?

CLARION. CLARION, ARE YOU PLANNING TO FRAME HIM FOR CRIMES?

OH, I *WISH* I'D THOUGHT OF THAT.

BUT WE DON'T EVEN *NEED* TO. LOOK, HE'S AN ARROGANT *BEAST*. I *BET* HE LEAVES SENSITIVE DOCUMENTS LYING AROUND IN HIS ROOMS.

AFTER ALL, WHO WOULD GO IN *THERE*?

YOU! YOU WOULD!

OH, NO. *YOU'RE* GOING TO DO THAT.

ARE YOU SURE THAT'S A GOOD IDEA?

OH YES. WE'VE GOT TWO *VERY* DIFFERENT SKILL SETS.

AND YOU'RE GOING TO NEED A *DISTRACTION* TO MAKE SURE HE DOESN'T *CATCH* YOU.

THIS ISN'T GOING TO BE A SCHEME ANYONE FORGETS IN A HURRY, IS IT?

RIGHT. YOU KNOW WHAT TO DO, YEAH?

OF COURSE. ANIMATE IT, MAKE IT SAY THE SCRIPT, DON'T LET IT STOP.

GO!

MUTTERMUTTERMUTTER

I'M TRYSIL HELDRITCH!

PFFT!

AND I SMELL LIKE HOT STICKY TRASH!

LAST NIGHT I HAD A BATH IN THE *SAUCE!* ENJOY!

THIS IS *SO MUCH* BETTER THAN I IMAGINED!

THAT'S IT, BOSS. YOU JUST STAY RIGHT THERE.

HAHAHA

I **WISH** I COULD STAY AND WATCH THE SHOW.

BUT THERE'S NO **TIME**.

Heldritch

HE LIVES LIKE **THIS**?

THIS IS **CARNAGE**.

IS THAT THE BRAZEN MANTICORE? AND . . .

ChefAuguste: Kitchen Hero,,

NO.

SOME 'FOUNDER' **HE** IS!

SO, TELL ME ALL ABOUT IT. WHAT DID YOU *GET*?

KEEP IT DOWN! I'VE GOT SECRETS!

STOP *TEASING* ME! SHOW ME THE *LOOT*!

WHAT AM I LOOKING AT?

SEE HIM? THERE, AT THE BACK? LOOKING LIKE HE'S BEEN KICKED?

THIS PROVES HE DIDN'T FOUND THE RESTAURANT.

IT SHOWS HE'S A *LIAR*, AND I BET HE'S EMBARRASSED ABOUT HIS PAST.

OOH, I BET HE'D *HATE* US KNOWING THAT.

COME ON, SHOW US THE PAPERS!

LOOK AT THIS ONE! LOOKS LIKE IT'S AN OLD **WILL**, LEAVING THE MANTICORE TO HELDRITCH.

BUT I'M PRETTY SURE THAT'S THE BOSS'S HANDWRITING.

THAT'S **TERRIBLE**. THIS ONE'S A LIST OF POLITICIANS, GOING BACK **DECADES**, WITH **PRICES** NEXT TO EACH ONE.

THINK THESE ARE **BRIBES**?

YEAH. HEY, HERE'S A SET OF NOTES FOR A **SPEECH** OR SOMETHING.

'TELL THEM THEY'RE IN DANGER FROM THE **TOWN** . . .' WHAT'S THIS ABOUT?

GIMME! I WANT TO SEE!

OH! **THIS** IS WHAT WE NEED!

LOOK, IT'S A **PROTECTION RACKET**. BUT WHO'S HE TAKING ADVANTAGE OF HERE?

OH. **SOUP**. HE'S A **MONSTER**.

HE'S CONVINCED THE **FAE** THAT HE'S KEEPING THEM SAFE FROM THE **TOWN**.

STOP IT, CLARI! THIS ISN'T THE TIME FOR JOKES.

I'M . . . NOT JOKING.

WHAT? BUT THE **FAE** AREN'T REAL!

PRETTY SURE THEY **ARE**. I KNOW A FEW OF 'EM. WE HANG OUT IN THE **WOODS** SOMETIMES.

YOU DON'T THINK . . . ?

THAT MEETING YOU OVERHEARD?

COULD THE FAE GIVE HIM *MAGIC*?

IT ALL MAKES SENSE NOW. HE'S TAKING THEIR **MAGIC** IN EXCHANGE FOR PRETENDING TO PROTECT THEM!

WE'VE GOT TO STOP HIM FROM DOING THINGS LIKE THIS.

IN THE MORNING, WE'RE GOING FOR A **WALK**.

'I NEED TO INTRODUCE YOU TO SOME . . .*PEOPLE*.'

THIS IS OUR **SPECIAL** MEETING PLACE. NOBODY EVER COMES HERE EXCEPT US.

IT'S WHERE WE GO WHEN **CLARION** WANTS TO DO SOMETHING **IMPORTANT**.

OR JUST SOMETHING THAT'LL **REALLY** GET US INTO TROUBLE.

MORNING, PAL! READY TO GO?

ALL READY! I BROUGHT SNACKS FOR THE JOURNEY.

SNACKS CAN *WAIT*. C'MON!

THIS FEELS LIKE AN **ADVENTURE**.

C'MON! THIS WAY!

I HOPE YOU KNOW WHAT YOU'RE DOING!

ALSO, SHE BROUGHT SNACKS. SEE, I **TOLD** YOU SHE'S NICE.

UM. HI. I BROUGHT CAKE.

DO THE **FAE** EVEN **EAT** CAKE?

OR AM **I** THE SNACK HERE?

THIS IS *PERMISSIBLE.* BE WELCOME.

THANK YOU?

CLARION AND FRIEND. YOU MAY *STAY.*

WE'VE BEEN TALKING FOR **HOURS**.

...SO HE'S NEVER **REWARDED** YOU FOR ALL THE POWERS YOU GIVE HIM?

HE SAYS WE *WILL* GET OUR REWARD.

BUT WE HAVE NOT HAD ONE YET.

BUT I THINK WE MIGHT **FINALLY** BE GETTING SOMEWHERE.

MAYBE YOU SHOULD GO AND **GET** THAT REWARD FROM HIM?

BECAUSE I'M PRETTY SURE HE OWES YOU **A LOT**.

WE WILL *CLAIM* WHAT IS OURS.

THAT'S MORE LIKE IT. NOW, LISTEN UP.

WE'VE GOT A **PLAN**.

YOU SHOULD COME TO THE TOWN **TOMORROW**.

TODAY'S THE DAY.

CHAPTER SIX:
BIG NIGHT

IF I WANT THE **BEST** INGREDIENTS, I HAVE TO BE HERE **EARLY**.

AND THIS? THIS **IS** THE BEST.

GOOD LUCK OUT THERE.

UH, THANKS!

OH, YEAH, THAT'S RIGHT.

UM.

ALSO, LITERALLY **EVERYONE** KNOWS ABOUT THE CONTEST NOW.

WHICH IS **FINE** AND NOT **STRESSFUL** AT ALL!

HEY! SOUP!

FRUIT FOR YOU!

HOW ARE YOU DOING, LOVE?

I'M FINE.

...I'M NOT FINE.

IT'S ALL SO MUCH PRESSURE, AND I FEEL LIKE EVERYONE IS **WATCHING** ME.

THERE'S *SO MUCH* RIDING ON THIS. FOR EVERYONE, NOT JUST FOR ME.

THAT MAKES IT SO MUCH MORE OF AN OPPORTUNITY.

YEAH?

YEAH. YOU WORK IN A **RESTAURANT**. YOU ALREADY COOK UNDER PRESSURE ALL THE TIME.

SO TRY TO HAVE *FUN* OUT THERE. THAT'S WHAT *REALLY* MATTERS.

I WILL. THANKS, SABINE.

YOU ALRIGHT? HAD A BUSY WEEK, HUH?

JUST A BIT, YEAH.

I SHOULD HAVE ASKED YOU TWO IF YOU WANTED TO BE PART OF ALL THIS.

YOU HELPED ME SEE WHAT WAS REALLY GOING ON.

NAH, WE DON'T GOT *TIME.* MESTON FOUND A BIG NEST OF **WORMS** AND THAT'S TAKEN UP ALL OUR DAYS.

UH, OKAY . . .

'ERE, TAKE THIS. 'S **NOT** WORMS.

IT'S SUGAR-CURED **TREEHOG** BELLY. USE IT TODAY AND THINK OF US OUT HERE, 'KAY?

I'M SURPRISED YOU EVEN BOTHERED TO TURN UP.

CHARNABEL JANSSON:
TOWN COUNCIL PRESIDENT

SHIP STRIPLEY:
HEAD OF THE TOURISM BOARD

MORVEN HOLMEN:
TRADE MAGNATE

YOU MAY GO TO YOUR STATIONS. WE'LL BE STARTING SOON.

LET'S HAVE A **FAIR** FIGHT TODAY, ALRIGHT?

YOU WILL EACH MAKE **ONE** DISH TO THE BEST OF YOUR ABILITIES.

ONE DISH, WHATEVER YOU *MOST* WANT TO SHARE WITH US.

WE WANT TO SEE SOMETHING *UNIQUE* AND *DELICIOUS.*

SOUP

SHOW US WHO YOU *REALLY* ARE.

YOU HAVE **SIX** HOURS. YOUR TIME STARTS . . . NOW!

SOUP!

THE PASTRY AND THE JELLY NEED TO **CHILL** FOR A WHILE.

NOW WHAT?

RIC

THIS **MIGHT** WORK.

SPLURCH!

THAT SEAWEED IS PACKED WITH **ALGINATE**. HIS PRESENTATION'S GOING TO BE TOUGH TO MATCH.

PLIP

SPHERIFICATION IS A GOOD TRICK. ESPECIALLY WHEN IT'S BOOSTED WITH **MAGIC**.

THAT'S ENOUGH.

THERE. BEHOLD MY **GENIUS**.

SPLORT

I'LL BE WITH YOU IN A MINUTE!

DON'T WAIT FOR HER. HONESTLY, YOU DON'T EVEN HAVE TO TASTE HER DISH.

OH, COME ON. JUST BECAUSE IT'S ENDANGERED DOESN'T MEAN IT'S GOOD.

I MEAN, **CHEF AUGUSTE** WOULD HAVE DONE SOMETHING SO MUCH *BETTER* WITH A CUT OF MEAT LIKE THAT.

HOW DO YOU KNOW *THAT* NAME?

THAT WAS . . . UNEXPECTED?

HIS FOOD WAS SO GOOD, THOUGH . . .

FINISH THE CONTEST!

WITH ONE OF OUR CONTESTANTS, AH, *INDISPOSED*, I'M NOT SURE THERE'S MUCH POINT?

SOUP IS THE WINNER!

NO.

NO? BUT YOU'VE WON. YOU DON'T HAVE AN OPPONENT.

NO! THAT'S NOT RIGHT!

OH NO, NOT AGAIN.

WE'VE COOKED FOR YOU.

FOR YOU.

YOU SHOULD RESPECT THAT AND AT LEAST TASTE IT.

FOOD ISN'T ART. IT'S MADE TO BE EATEN. SHARED.

YES, THIS WAS A CONTEST ABOUT STOPPING HIS INJUSTICE, AND THAT'S IMPORTANT.

BUT IT'S NOT JUST ABOUT THAT, IS IT?

IT'S ABOUT FOOD TOO. MINE VERSUS HIS. DOESN'T THAT MEAN ANYTHING?

WHAT I MEAN IS, AFTER ALL HE SAID ABOUT ME, I *NEED* TO KNOW THAT I'M *BETTER* THAN HELDRITCH.

THAT WHAT EVERYONE HELPED ME MAKE IS *BETTER*.

SO NO, YOU'RE **WRONG**.

WE'VE COOKED FOR YOU, AND YOU SHOULD JUDGE OUR DISHES *FAIRLY*.

THERE'S A *LOT* GOING ON WITH THIS. SO MANY **DIFFERENT** IDEAS THAT SHOULD *NOT* BE COMING TOGETHER THIS WELL.

IT'S REMARKABLE. THERE'S SUCH A CLEAR **VOICE** TYING IT TOGETHER.

CAN I HAVE SECONDS?

'S SO MUCH FUN. WHAT D'YOU CALL IT?

LET'S CALL IT...
HELDRITCH'S FOLLY.

HERBED PASTRY SHELL.

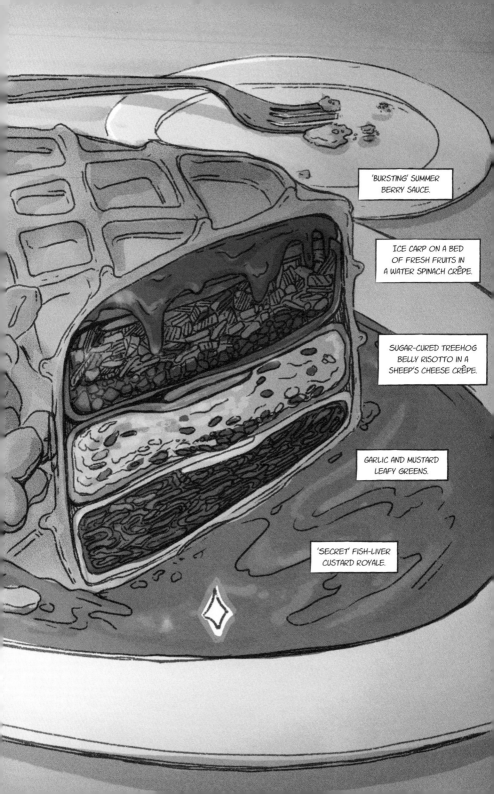

'BURSTING' SUMMER
BERRY SAUCE.

ICE CARP ON A BED
OF FRESH FRUITS IN
A WATER SPINACH CRÊPE.

SUGAR-CURED TREEHOG
BELLY RISOTTO IN A
SHEEP'S CHEESE CRÊPE.

GARLIC AND MUSTARD
LEAFY GREENS.

'SECRET' FISH-LIVER
CUSTARD ROYALE.

ONE MORE THING, **CHEF**.

WITH HELDRITCH *GONE*, THERE'S A VACANCY AT THE VERY TOP OF THE FOOD CHAIN.

WE COULD USE A NEW **CELEBRITY CHEF**. A CULINARY *FIGUREHEAD*. AN AMBASSADOR FOR OUR TOWN.

SO, HOW ABOUT IT, CHEF?

ME? TAKE OVER THE MANTICORE?

NO, THANK YOU.

WHY DOES SHE KEEP DOING THIS?

I DON'T THINK THE MANTICORE NEEDS A BIG, FAMOUS OWNER.

I THINK IT COULD BE SO MUCH MORE.

EPILOGUE:
THE NEW MANTICORE

IT'S BEEN A FEW MONTHS SINCE THE CONTEST.

*THINGS ARE **DIFFERENT** AT THE MANTICORE NOW.*

NOBODY SHOULD BE SHUT OUT OF COOKING HOW THEY WANT.

THIS IS FOR ALL OF THEM.

BUT I CAN'T GO **BACK** TO JUST COOKING LIKE I USED TO.

I'VE CHANGED TOO MUCH.

READY TO GO?

AND THEN I COME **HOME** AND I **COOK** FOR THE PEOPLE I CARE ABOUT.

AND SOMETIMES, SO DOES **CLARION**.

. . . THEY'RE **LEARNING**.

CLARI, IT'S IN YOUR EARS!

WE **SHARE** OUR WORLDS.

WE MADE *THIS?*

MMF!

TOGETHER, WE CAN DO **ANYTHING**.

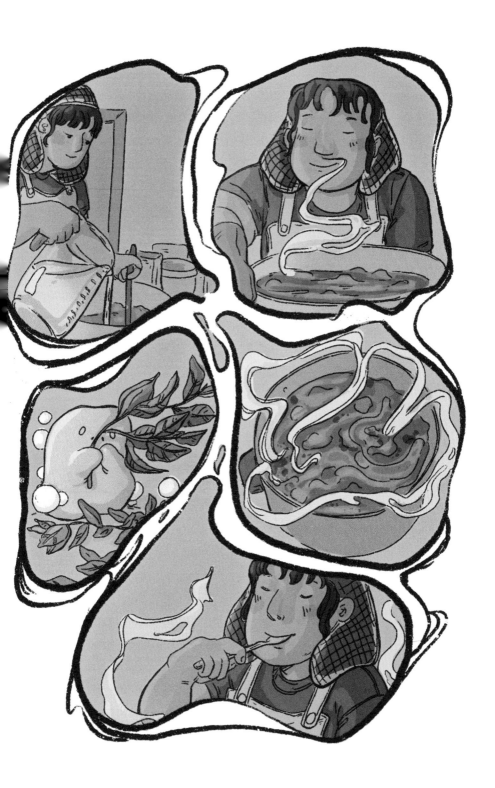

SMELLS *GOOD*.

HERE. TRY SOME.

TASTES GOOD TOO! IS THAT GOING ON THE *MENU* TONIGHT?

NO . . .

ABOUT THE CREATORS

OLIVER GERLACH is a writer, escaped chef and doctor of classics, living and working in Edinburgh, Scotland. His work can be found in places including 2000 AD's *Mega City Max* and the GLAAD and Ringo award-winning anthology *Young Men In Love*. On the rare occasions when he is not writing, Oliver can be found teaching and selling board and role-playing games. He still can't quite believe he gets to do both of these for a living. He probably spends too much time in the kitchen too. *The Restaurant at the Edge of the World* is his debut graphic novel.

KELSI JO SILVA is an American illustrator and artist based out of Denver, Colorado. After graduating from the Rocky Mountain College of Art and Design with a BA in illustration, Kelsi went straight into formulating a creative career. They've worked on a number of projects, most notably the Ela Cat children's series with Good Luck Black Cat books, the first of which was awarded a MoonBeam Award for illustration. Online, Kelsi is most known for her depictions of women in loving relationships and sapphic redesigns of Greek mythos.